HELLO, CROW!

by CANDACE SAVAGE

illustrated by CHELSEA O'BYRNE

DAVID SUZUKI INSTITUTE

GREYSTONE KIDS

GREYSTONE BOOKS • VANCOUVER/BERKELEY

Franny was a dreamer.
That's what her dad said.

A dreamer didn't think about what
she was doing and left things in a mess.

"If only you would learn to pay attention,"
he said. "What am I going to do with you,
my Franny Featherhead?"

But Franny *was* paying attention.

She was watching the shadows of the tree outside the window dance around the room.

She was listening to the cries of the birds in the branches, calling her to come outside, into the big, wild world.

"Here you go," her dad said with a sigh and kissed the
top of her head. "A little something for your adventure."

Franny skipped down the steps and into the bright morning air.
Every bug, every leaf, every petal was shimmering with wonder.

After a while, she sat on her favorite
rock and started to eat her lunch.

Crumbs went flying in every direction,
but she didn't notice them. She was
too busy watching the big, black bird
that was coming toward her.

The bird kept waddling closer:

Hop, hop, stop.

Hop, hop.

Whenever he stopped, he tilted
his head and looked at Franny.

He looked at the crumbs
around her feet.

Closer he hopped,
and closer.

Franny sat completely still. She hardly dared to breathe.
He was so close she could have reached over and touched
his wings, but she didn't.

"Hello, Crow," she whispered, because she knew that's who he was.
"I am very pleased to make your acquaintance."

When the crow had poked and prodded in the grass and eaten every last crumb, he fixed one round eye on Franny and gave her a little nod.

Then, with a rush of rustling feathers, he leaped into the sky and was gone.

"He's beautiful and shiny," she told her dad that evening,
"and he's my friend, and he likes sandwiches, same as me,
and you should come meet him, and—"

Her dad looked up from what he was doing.

"Where do you get all your
featherbrained ideas?"
he said and ruffled her hair.

"You know as well as I do that
you can't have a crow for a friend.
Now go take off those muddy shoes
and get ready for dinner."

The next morning, Franny had a problem. She was going to
need two sandwiches, one for herself and one for the crow.
But she knew without even asking that her father would say, "no."

"I'll make my own lunch this morning," she called to him.
"And don't worry. I won't make a mess."

Franny was dressed and ready to go by the time her dad got up.

Franny thought of a dozen different ways to pass the time while she waited, but there was no sign of her friend.

After a while, she sat on her rock and ate her lunch. Alone.

And then suddenly, there
he was, rushing towards her,
not hopping this time but flying,
swooping low across the lawn.

He landed with a thump and
a flourish right beside her.

"Caw, caw," shouted the
crow with a little bow.

"Caw, caw," shouted Franny.
"I am happy to see you, too."

From then on, every day
was full of surprises.

When Franny told her dad about everything that had happened, he laughed and gave her a little hug.

"And then I suppose you flapped your wings and flew away with him?"

"No, Dad, listen to me," she protested, but he didn't seem to hear.

How would she ever get him to believe her?

And then the crow did something so wonderful that even Franny could hardly believe it was true. He brought her a gift.

He left it on top of her favorite rock
where she was sure to find it.

Next came a red bead. A few days later, a green pebble. Then, a tiny silver heart. One by one, Franny gathered up all the presents and carried them home with her.

"It's simple," she told her father. "Crow loves me, and I love him, too, and that's why he brings me presents, and—"

But her dad just shook his head. "I don't know where you found all this trash," he said wearily, "but this silliness has to stop."

Franny drew herself up to her full height and folded her arms across her chest. "These are treasures, not trash," she said firmly. "You need to come with me. I am going to prove to you that my new friend is real."

So Franny took her dad by the hand and half-led and half-dragged him to her favorite rock. "Come on, Crow," she thought to herself. "This is important."

They waited and waited and waited.

"That's it," her dad said at last. "Come on, time to go. I know you want to believe—"

But before he could say another word, a glossy black bird came swooping down out of nowhere and landed, plop, on Franny's head.

"Hello, Crow," said Franny.

"My word!" her father said.

From that moment on, Franny's dad did his best to pay attention to what she said.

"And Franny, I am sorry that I called you a featherhead."

"Oh, don't be sorry," she reassured him. "I like being a featherhead, just like my new friend."

"Caw, caw, caw," shouted the crow.

"See, he agrees," said Franny, and she and her dad both laughed.

CURIOUS ABOUT CROWS

Is it a crow?

Is the bird shiny and black all over, even its beak and feet? Does it caw and croak in a loud, harsh voice? If the answer is "yes" to both these questions, then hooray! You have seen a crow or its larger cousin, a raven.

What do crows eat?

In the wild, crows eat all sorts of things, including fruit, nuts, insects, eggs, nestlings, and garbage. If you want to feed crows, try offering them peanuts in the shell. Choose a place where you often see crows and set the food out at around the same time every day. Be patient. It may take a long time before the crows decide it's safe to come down and eat.

Can people and crows be friends?

Crows are very smart, and they are always learning new things. Although they are naturally jumpy and fearful, they can learn to trust people who give them food. Sometimes, like the crow in the story, these brainy birds even bring presents, as if to say "thanks" or "give me more!" But do they actually like or love their human helpers? What do you think?

For Asha and Laurel. — C. S.

For T.H., the sweetest featherhead I know. — C. O.

Text copyright © 2019 by Candace Savage
Illustrations copyright © 2019 by Chelsea O'Byrne

First published in the U.K. in 2020

19 20 21 22 23 5 4 3 2 1

All rights reserved. No part of this book may be reproduced, stored in a retrieval system or transmitted,
in any form or by any means, without the prior written consent of the publisher or a license from
The Canadian Copyright Licensing Agency (Access Copyright). For a copyright license, visit accesscopyright.ca
or call toll free to 1-800-893-5777.

Greystone Kids / Greystone Books Ltd.
greystonebooks.com

David Suzuki Institute
219—2211 West 4th Avenue
Vancouver, BC V6K 4S2

Cataloguing data available from Library and Archives Canada
ISBN 978-1-77164-444-0 (cloth)
ISBN 978-1-77164-445-7 (epub)
ISBN 978-1-77164-446-4 (ePDF)

MIX
Paper from
responsible sources
FSC® C012700

Editing by Kallie George
Copy editing by Antonia Banyard
Jacket and text design by Sara Gillingham Studio
Jacket illustration by Chelsea O'Byrne

Printed and bound in Malaysia on ancient-forest-friendly paper by Tien Wah Press

Greystone Books gratefully acknowledges the Musqueam, Squamish, and Tsleil-Waututh peoples
on whose land our office is located.

Greystone Books thanks the Canada Council for the Arts, the British Columbia Arts Council,
the Province of British Columbia through the Book Publishing Tax Credit, and the Government of Canada
for supporting our publishing activities.

 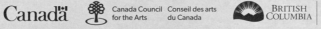 

Canada

Canada Council
for the Arts

Conseil des arts
du Canada

BRITISH
COLUMBIA

BRITISH COLUMBIA
ARTS COUNCIL
An agency of the Province of British Columbia

The David Suzuki Institute is a non-profit organization founded in 2010 to stimulate debate and action
on environmental issues. The Institute and the David Suzuki Foundation both work to advance awareness
of environmental issues important to all Canadians.

We invite you to support the activities of the Institute. For more information please contact us at:

David Suzuki Institute
info@davidsuzukiinstitute.org
604-742-2899
davidsuzukiinstitute.org

Cheques can be made payable to The David Suzuki Institute.

**DAVID
SUZUKI
INSTITUTE**